& the
# WELSH BLACK
# CATTLE

The Welsh Black Cattle Society
www.welshblackcattlesociety.com

WIL

& the

WELSH BLACK CATTLE

PHIL OKWEDY

illustrated by

PETER STEVENSON

Gomer

First published in 2018 by Gomer Press,
Llandysul, Ceredigion SA44 4JL

ISBN 978 1 78562 234 2
A CIP record for this title is available
from the British Library.

This book is published with the financial support of the
Welsh Books Council.

Printed and bound in Wales at
Gomer Press, Llandysul, Ceredigion
www.gomer.co.uk

A Fairy Dog

Not all that long ago, but before there were banks or trains, and when it was the drovers rather than the telegraph wires that carried the news from place to place, there were three brothers who each owned a share of a small farm near Moylgrove, in the Wild, Wild West of Wales.

Now, just as in that other Wild West, the one across the Atlantic Ocean where cowboys rode horses and carried six shooters, people in Wales also counted their wealth in cattle back then. But the brothers' farm was a small place, a poor place. Not much more than a couple of oxen, a house where the rain came through the roof and a yard where the grass grew up through the cracks. Each evening when the brothers sat down to their miserable meal in the damp kitchen, the blessing was always the same:

Arglwydd annwyl! Dyma fwyd.
Cawl sur a bara llwyd.
Good Lord! What a spread.
Sour broth and mouldy bread.

It was hardly surprising, then, that each of the brothers had thought of a plan for improving his fortunes. Each wanted to marry Megan, the only daughter of the rich farmer who lived on the next-door farm.

Two of these brothers were evil, venomous toads. Tomos, the eldest, was lazy. Sion, the middle brother, was sly. Neither did much work on the farm. Together they made a pact. Whichever one of them married Megan, she would cook and clean for them both and do all the chores on the farm too. Then, when her father died, that farm would also be theirs.

It was only the youngest brother, Wil, who wanted to marry Megan for love. Megan, whose hair was the colour of ripening wheat. Megan, whose eyes were as blue as a swallow's wing. Megan, whose lips were as red as the geraniums that grew in the window box beneath her window.

Of course, Megan's father knew none of this and didn't know which of the brothers to choose for his beloved daughter. So, he set them a challenge.

To each he gave a small brown calf, saying, 'Whoever gets the best price for their calf by the time of Eglwyswrw Fair in the autumn shall marry my daughter.'

Well, Tomos was so lazy that he didn't bother feeding his little calf at all. Within two weeks it had starved to death. As for Sion, he was so sly, always poking his nose into other people's business, that he didn't have much time to care for his calf properly. The poor thing was all skin and bones. It was only Wil's calf that put on flesh and muscle, put on weight. It seemed certain that he would get the best price. And that was just as well. For as Wil loved Megan, Megan loved Wil.

Unknown to anyone, the two of them had been meeting in secret for many months.

One summer evening, a month or two after Wil had been given the calf, they were sitting in the porch of the church. Megan was knitting socks and asking how the calf was doing. The socks were to sell to drovers. For unlike the cowboys in America who rode horses, Welsh drovers walked. Looking after their feet was important. They would grease them with pig fat before pulling on long socks. Then, when they put on their wooden clogs, their feet could slide about so they wouldn't get blisters. And Megan was asking after the calf because she wanted Wil to win. He was assuring her all was well while constantly trying to steal kisses. In order to put him off – she was afraid she was going to drop a stitch – Megan began to tell Wil a story about a strange thing that had happened the week before.

She was in the farmyard collecting hen's eggs when she heard whining out in the lane. She went to investigate and sure enough, there was a little dog pressed up against the hedge, sopping wet and whimpering. Instantly, she recognised it as a drover's dog.

It was a corgi, and she knew the drovers used them as their herding dogs. A corgi was small enough to run in and nip a dawdling beast on the leg and get out quickly before it was kicked. She had heard too that when the drovers reached the Welsh border on their way back from selling the cattle in England, they often sent their dogs on ahead of them. The dog would revisit all the inns that it had been to with its master on the outward journey, where it would be fed and watered again. When the dog arrived home, the drover's family would know that he was not many days behind and so could prepare everything to welcome him back.

Sweeping the dog up in her apron, Megan had nothing but kindness in her heart for the poor little creature as she turned back towards the house. Even so, she'd only run a few steps when she gave a little shudder. Suddenly, she remembered another story about a drover's dog.

It was a cousin who'd found it, but the cousin had no love for the drovers in her heart. You see, when the drover collected the one or two beasts that a poor farmer might let go each year, no money changed hands then. He collected from many such farmers, and when he had a large enough herd, he would drive them to the markets in England where he would sell them. Only then would he return, visiting each poor farmer and paying him for his animals. That money might be the only hard cash that a family would see all year.

Unfortunately, the drover that the cousin's family had done business with never returned. That had been a hard winter. A cold winter. A hungry winter. So when the cousin found the little dog, she took it home all right. She took it home and tied it up in a dark passage. Each time one of the family walked past, they would shout at that little dog. Kick it. Beat it.

When there was a knock on the door several days later, the cousin expected to find a drover in a wide-brimmed hat and a long coat with secret pockets for hiding money in standing there. Instead, there was a crowd of little old men dressed in reds and greens with long, gangly arms and long, bony fingers.

'What would you have for treating our dog thus?' growled one of them, stepping forward. 'Would you travel above the wind, mid-wind or beneath the wind?'

The cousin had no desire for her feet to leave the earth at all. So without hesitation, and despite the shock of finding the *Tylwyth Teg* on her doorstep, she said, 'Beneath the wind.'

No sooner had she uttered those words than long, bony fingers reached out and pinched her by the nostril, the lip, the eyelid. Bony hands took fistfuls of hair and she was dragged screaming through hedge and thicket, over rock face and scree, until she was cut and battered and bruised and half dead.

Remembering this, there was a little fear as well as kindness in Megan's heart as she walked back through the farmyard. Of course, she had no intention of treating the little dog badly. She made it a bed by the range. Fed it. Talked to it. Petted it.

Sure enough, when there was a knock on the door several days later, Megan opened it to find not a drover, but that crowd of little old men dressed in reds and greens with long, gangly arms and long, bony fingers.

'What would you have for treating our dog thus, a clean yard or a dirty yard?'

At this point in her story, Megan fell silent.

For a moment, the only sound in the porch was the click-clack of wooden knitting needles.

'Well,' said Wil, when it was clear she was going to say no more. 'What did you say? A clean yard or a dirty yard?'

Megan smiled. 'I'm not telling.'

'Oh, come on! You can't just stop there. What did you say to the *Tylwyth Teg*? A clean yard or a dirty yard?'

Megan smiled some more. 'I'm not telling.'

'It's like that, is it? Well, you will tell me.' Laughing, Wil reached out, grabbed her and began tickling. 'Now tell me, what did you say to the *Tylwyth Teg*? A clean yard or a dirty yard?'

Squirming out of his grasp, she giggled, 'I'm not telling.'

Just then, they heard the squeal of the churchyard gate.

They peered out into the purpling dusk. Two figures were walking through the graves as a bat flew in erratic circles above their heads. The figures stopped in the gathering shadows beneath the yew tree. They appeared to reach up, break off branches of yew and put them in

9

a sack. Then, Megan and Wil watched as the two figures made their way back through the grave stones.

The churchyard gate clanged shut.

'Come on then, tell me. What did you say to the *Tylwyth Teg*? A clean yard or a dirty yard?'

Wil seized hold of Megan again and there was more tickling, squirming, giggling.

'I'm not telling,' she said. And, what with one thing and another, they forgot all about the two figures walking through the grave stones.

That is until two days later, when Wil walked into the shed to feed his little calf only to find it lying on its side, stiff as a board. Dead!

At first, he couldn't understand it and stood there, scratching his head. Then he noticed the yew twigs in the feeding trough. Well, Wil knew yew was fatal to cattle. But if he jumped to any conclusions as to how it had got into the feeding trough, he didn't act on them. Instead, he took out the little knife he always kept in his pocket and began to skin the calf. When he was finished, he took the hide and put it in a safe place where it could dry out.

Summer droned on and Wil and Megan met as often as they could in the porch of the church. Megan always asked how the calf was doing. Wil always replied that it was doing just fine and asked her what she had said to the *Tylwyth Teg*, 'A clean yard or a dirty yard?'

But she only ever answered, 'I'm not telling.'

Summer gave way to autumn and the day of Eglwyswrw Fair arrived. It was a cold November morning as Sion slipped the halter over his skinny calf's head. Stepping out for the fair, he whistled a happy little tune, safe in the knowledge that he was going to win the challenge and so Megan's hand in marriage. After all, there were no other calves left alive.

The usual sights met him as he arrived in Eglwyswrw. The streets were jam packed with hundreds of coal-black cattle – Welsh Black cattle. Steam rose off their backs, billowed from their mouths and wafted up from the hoof-deep manure in which they stood. Dogs, large collies as well as corgis, ran among the beasts' legs. The drovers, clustered in twos and threes, wearing their wide-brimmed hats and long coats with deep pockets for hiding money in, smoked and laughed and did deals with each other.

There were other men too. For just as in that other Wild West on the far side of the Atlantic Ocean, the cattle must be caught before they could set off on the drive. Not for branding with hot irons, as was the case in America, but for shoeing. It might be as much as a three-hundred-mile walk to the cattle markets in England, so the animals' feet must be protected.

Where the American cowboys used a lasso to catch their beasts, here it was big men like Deio from Hendy who did the catching. Men who today would be playing prop forward for Wales would step forward, catch a beast by its horns, run a few steps, then twist its neck and fell it like a child. Then others would run out, tie the four feet together and prop them up on a forked stick, ready for shoeing. The shoes themselves were called cues and eight rather than four were needed for the cloven hooves of a cow.

A large flock of geese was driven through hot tar and then a mixture of sand and shells so that they too had 'shoes'. Down a side street, the cobbler was busy making boots for the pigs that would also be making the journey.

Among all the familiar sights that morning, there was one that was not. He was an old man whom Sion had never seen before. His hat was pulled down so low it almost hid his eyes and his great, white beard was as woolly as a sheep would be if it had somehow avoided shearing for several years. His coat was tied up with string and around his neck hung hundreds and hundreds of bootlaces.

All day long he walked about the fair shouting, "*Rhics, rhocs, careion, clocs. Rhics, rhocs, careion, clocs,*' selling those bootlaces for a penny a pair.

By the end of the day, Sion had sold his calf, and so went to see Megan's father in his study. Her father glared at him from across the desk as Sion lay down three pounds on the shiny wooden surface. He had just taken Sion's hand to shake it when there was a knock on the door.

'Excuse me, Father, but there is a gentleman here looking for lodgings for the night.'

The farmer smiled at his only daughter. 'Well, you see to it, *cariad*.'

'I would, Father, but he says he wants you to look after his money until the morning.'

'Money, is it? Then we better count it now. I don't want to be accused of thieving in the morning! Come in, come in,' he beckoned.

Into the study walked the old man with the woolly beard who'd been selling bootlaces at the fair. The bag of pennies he'd collected was poured out onto the desk top and they counted out three pounds. Three pounds and 12 pennies. Three pounds and a shilling.

Just as the very last penny was placed on the very last pile, the old man jumped up, whipped off his hat, pulled off his great white woolly beard and Wil exclaimed, 'There. That's how much I got for my calf!'

You could have heard a very small pin drop.

'Well, well. Here's a quandary now,' Megan's father said, staring sternly at the two young men.

'I was just about shaking your hand and

14

that's sealing a bargain,' he muttered to Sion. 'But you have clearly won the challenge,' he said, turning to Wil.

'This is going to take some thought,' he said, smiling at Megan as he shook his head. And, perhaps because he was in no hurry to lose his only daughter, he said, 'I shall let you know which of you will marry my daughter, but not until next year's Eglwyswrw Fair.'

2

Three Brothers
of Moylgrove

Autumn gave way to winter. Short, dark days made it harder for Wil and Megan to meet, but when they did Wil always asked the same question:

'What did you say to the *Tylwyth Teg*? A clean yard or a dirty yard?'

But Megan only ever answered, 'I'm not telling.'

Snowdrops and primroses appeared in the hedgerows as winter made way for spring. One day in early March found Wil up on the top field, driving the oxen before the plough, when one of the beasts suddenly stopped, coughed, and fell down dead.

Poor Wil was beside himself. The oxen represented the greatest part of the farm's wealth, and now half of it was gone.

But if Wil had been upset, his brothers were

furious when they heard of the animal's death. They blamed Wil, as though he had killed the beast on purpose, and would hear no excuses. Harsh words soon turned to harsh blows as they ploughed into Wil with fists and hobnail boots until he lay unconscious on the kitchen floor in a pool of his own blood.

Maybe they'd been planning it all along, or maybe it only occurred to them then, but if they got rid of Wil, Sion would be free to marry Megan.

So they bundled Wil into an old grain sack and tied it up. Then, between them, they dragged it up and over the ploughed field to the cliffs above Ceibwr Bay. From there they tossed the sack out into the void, and turned for home, never expecting to see their brother again.

Meanwhile, the sack plummeted towards the sea like a meteor. When it hit the water, it was like hitting stone. The bottom of the sack split open, sending Wil plunging down into the freezing depths. Coughing and sputtering, he fought his way to the surface, only to be caught by a huge wave that dumped him down on the pebble beach below the cliffs.

Wil lay there gasping for breath like a landed fish. His mind reeled with murderous thoughts. Then with thoughts of revenge as an idea came to him. Clambering back up the cliff, he crossed the ploughed field, skinned the dead ox with his little knife and set off to see Megan.

By the time he reached her house it was dark, but he soon found the red geraniums in the window box beneath her window. He threw small stones against the glass until she opened it.

'My brothers tried to kill me. I'd never get away with it if I tried to do the same to them. So, I'm going away to seek enough of a fortune to buy them out of their share of the farm. It shouldn't take that much. They are greedy and stupid. They might complain later, but possession is nine-tenths of the law. Will you wait for me?'

'Of course.'

'Then, as we may not see each other until the Eglwyswrw Fair, will you tell me what you said to the *Tylwyth Teg*, a clean yard or a dirty yard?'

Megan smiled. 'I'm not telling.'

With those words ringing in his ears, Wil set off into the night.

Next morning found him in Cardigan where he sold the ox hide for a handful of copper and silver coins. It wasn't enough to buy his brothers out yet, but it was a start.

While Wil awaited a chance to turn his coins into something more, he slept rough. His hair became matted with mud and twigs. His beard grew long, his nails black and broken. His clothes turned to rags.

One morning, after having slept rough on the banks of the River Teifi, Wil awoke to find a cormorant drying its wings in the sun. At least drying one of them, for the other was broken and hung limp.

To Wil's surprise, far from shying away, the bird allowed him to handle it, and he soon fashioned a splint for its broken wing out of twigs and seaweed.

For one week, two weeks, three weeks, Wil tended the bird. It ate what he ate, slept where he slept. Then, during the fourth week, as the bird grew stronger and the splint came off, he had an idea of how to turn his handful of

coins into something more. He hid the money in three separate piles beneath the town walls. Then, he tucked the bird under his arm and headed for Cardigan market.

It was full of Cardi women in tall hats and shawls, and men with flat caps and moustaches. When they saw Wil with his long beard, ragged clothes and a big black bird under his arm, they took him for some kind of idiot.

'What you got there, boy, a magic bird is it?' asked one old man.

'As a matter of fact, it is.'

'Oh! Well then, I'll give you a pound for it,' laughed another.

'A pound!' said Wil. 'I can find a pound a day with this bird.'

'Get away with you,' said the first old man.

'Suit yourself,' said Wil.

'Well, if it really is magic, prove it!' demanded the second old man.

'Very well.'

By now quite a crowd had gathered and Wil led them down the High Street and then to St Mary's Church.

'If there's treasure here, the bird will cry out,' he said. But as he knelt on the grass outside the vestibule, the bird remained silent.

The same thing happened at the Castle gate, and when the bird still made no noise at the bridge, the crowd began to jeer.

Undeterred, Wil crossed to the path that led beneath the town walls. This time, as he knelt he gave the cormorant a squeeze:

'Cak-cak-cak-cak-cak', the bird cried. And when Wil pulled out an assortment of copper and silver coins from a clump of coltsfoot, a gasp went up from the crowd.

When Wil again pulled out an assortment of copper and silver coins from a patch of periwinkle, someone shouted out: 'I'll give you five pounds for that bird.'

And when it happened for a third time, a bidding war started:

'I'll give you ten.'

'Twenty.'

'Fifty!'

In the end, Wil sold the bird to an old Cardigan miser for a hundred pounds, which was given to him in the form of five gold coins in a leather pouch that he could attach to his belt.

Then, he took his handful of copper and silver coins and used them to pay for a bath, new clothes, a haircut and a shave. After that, he left town pretty sharpish before it was discovered that that was no magic bird at all.

Now, as Wil walked back towards Moylgrove, he had enough to buy his brothers out. Two gold coins each should do it and there'd be one left over to replace the dead ox. Although, how much better it would be if he could turn it into a little more. Then he could fix the hole in the roof where the rain came in. He could buy his bride a new dress as a wedding present. A blue one to match her eyes.

Thinking of Megan made him wonder again what she had said to the *Tylwyth Teg*, a clean yard or a dirty yard? And how she only ever answered, 'I'm not telling.'

So Wil turned away from Moylgrove and began to head inland towards the Preseli Hills where he hoped to find a chance of turning his five gold coins into something more.

Public Enemy No.1

PART 1

Have you ever heard of Al Capone? He was an American gangster who ran the corrupt city of Chicago in the 1920s and 30s. He'd never been a drover and he certainly wasn't Welsh, but his right-hand man, Llewelyn Murray Humphreys or Murray the Hump, was.

Llewelyn's parents, Bryan and Ann Humphreys, had been tenants on a small farm up in the hills above Carno in Powys. It was hard to make a living on an isolated hilltop farm at the end of the nineteenth century. It seemed that the landlords were always putting up the rent. Llewelyn's father took whatever work he could in order to keep a roof over his young bride's head.

Among the many jobs he did was droving. Perhaps it was while he was travelling the country helping to drive herds of coal-black Welsh Black cattle to the meat markets in England that he heard about a land of opportunity. A place, it was said, where a family might make a new start. That land was America and it was to America, leaving behind all they had known and loved in Wales, that Llewelyn's parents emigrated in the 1890s. Llewelyn himself was born a short while later.

When they arrived in America, Llewelyn's father, Bryan, took his young family to the city of Chicago. He took them there because it was where the cattle that were driven across the great prairie grass lands of the American West were taken. Here, hoof-deep in manure, they were kept in acres of holding pens until they were finally put on trains and transported to feed the people in the cities of the eastern United States.

It seems it was Bryan's intention to use the skills he had learnt as a drover in Wales to get work as a cowboy in America.

3

The Fairy Cow

The next morning found Wil walking down a narrow lane beneath the Preseli Hills. Summer was in full swing. The hedgerows were heavy with purple foxgloves that buzzed with visiting bees. He rounded a bend to find an old, white-washed Pembrokeshire cottage with a tin roof on one side of the lane and, on the other, a stone-walled enclosure from which five coal-black Welsh Black cattle eyed him suspiciously. However, it was neither of these things that caught his attention, but the old man sitting in the doorway of the cottage. Great, fat tears were rolling down his cheeks and he was sharpening a wicked-looking knife on the edge of the slate step.

'Whatever is the matter?' asked Wil.

'It's them cattle there,' the old man said pointing with the knife and shaking his head. 'I used to be a drover, see, and those cattle, they were my pension. Been fattening them

26

26

up all winter. Was going to drive them to London myself, live the rest of my life on the price I got for them. But my hip's gone. Knee too, as it happens, so I can't take them. And there's no one else. So there's nothing for it but to slaughter them and salt the beef. Shame though it is.'

'I could take them,' Wil said, seeing a chance to turn his five coins into something more.

'Ah! It's not as simple as that. They're not just any old cattle, you know.'

'What do mean?' asked Wil.

'Well, sit a while and I'll tell you...'

The old man began: 'Lost amongst the creases and folds of the hills above Aberdovey is a small lake, Llyn Barfog, the Bearded Lake. It is said that each evening a group of fairy wives, the *Gwragedd Annwn*, gather there on its shores. Dressed in green, their long silver hair hanging down their backs, they come with their milk-white hounds and their herds of milk-white fairy cows.

So, when there was a knock on the door of the small farmhouse nearest the lake one morning, and the farmer opened it to find a woman dressed in green with long silver hair, he didn't need to ask who she was. And when she asked for something to eat, he didn't hesitate, but invited her in to share the meagre breakfast his wife had just prepared.

The woman ate but said nothing until she'd finished. Then, she rose to her full height and said, '*Oherwydd eich caredigrwydd, byddwch yn ffynnu* – for being kind, you will prosper,' and left without another word.

The farmer paid little attention to the woman's words until that evening, when he went to fetch his own cows in, and found there was a milk-white fairy cow grazing amongst them. When he brought the others into the shed to milk, the milk-white fairy cow followed. And, when it came her turn to be milked, what milk she gave. So rich, so creamy. In time, what butter, what cheese the farmer found could be made from that milk. In more time, what calves came from that milk-white fairy cow, calves that had calves of their own, so that in even more time, the farmer had herds and herds of the milk-white fairy cows. He grew rich and prosperous and famous throughout the area. From being a sickly stick of a man dressed in patched and ragged clothes, he grew healthy and plump and wore new tweed suits with yellow cravats tucked into the neck of his shirt.

But with riches did not come wisdom. Instead of gratitude came greed. When the milk-white fairy cow grew too old to give milk or provide any more calves, rather than putting her out to pasture, the farmer determined to squeeze the last bit of profit out of the beast. To this end, he began fattening her up for the slaughter.

When the day came, the yard was full of people come from far and wide to see the end of the now monstrously fat cow. The farmer brought her out through the crowds and tied her to a post. She lowed mournfully and gazed all about with huge, watery brown eyes. But if others felt some sympathy, the farmer felt none. All he could think of was how much he would make from the rib, the loin and the rump.

Then the butcher slipped on his apron, rolled up his sleeves and stepped forward. He raised the cudgel high above his head and, with all his might, brought it down between the cow's ears and felled her.

The moment her head struck the ground, a cry went up, 'Aargh!'

Every head turned to find its source.

On a crag high above the lake stood a figure dressed in green, her long silver hair windswept behind her. '*Codwch! Dewch adre.*'

With those words echoing around the hills, the milk-white fairy cow rose from the dead and began to make her way out of the yard and up the hill towards the lake. But she did not go alone. From all over the farm she was joined by her off-spring until there was an unbroken white line of cattle snaking their way up the hill towards the lake. The farmer tried his best to stop them, but could do nothing. One by one the fairy cattle disappeared beneath the waters of the lake until all were gone – all except one, and that was a little calf that had turned from milk-white to coal-black.'

'And it's that little calf that those beasts over there are descended from,' the old man said, waving the knife in the direction of the black cattle in the stone enclosure.

Wil looked from the old man sitting on his doorstep to the animals and back again. 'That's a good story, but I hope it doesn't put the price of the cattle up! Now, how much do you want for them?'

After some bargaining, they agreed on a price: five gold coins for five black cattle. Wil emptied his leather pouch, gave the coins to the old man and set off to drive those cattle.

Wil drove those cattle through the wind and the rain, the sunshine and the showers. He drove them from Puncheston to Pwll-trap, Carmarthen to Llandeilo, around the Beacons and up the Vale of Neath. He drove them through swollen rivers, across misty mountain tops and down steep-sided valleys where ravens tumbled overhead. And as he drove them, he acquired the attire of a drover: the long coat with deep pockets for hiding money in, the wide-brimmed hat and a twisted stick he cut from an old ash tree. He drove them through the lowlands where the buttercups grow, and the uplands, around peat bog and bracken.

And, by hook and by crook, and by the art and mystery that was the drover's trade, he drove those cattle up the London road to the fattening grounds, and then on into London itself and Smithfield Market, where he sold them for a fine profit.

Now the leather purse on his hip was half full of gold coins. Enough to buy his brothers out. Enough to replace the dead ox and fix the hole in the farm house roof. Enough to buy Megan a blue dress, a new dresser for the kitchen, and a milk cow and butter churn for her to turn. She'd like that, he thought.

Thinking of Megan made him wonder again what she had said to the *Tylwyth Teg*, a clean yard or a dirty yard? And how she only ever answered, 'I'm not telling.'

So, with the coins jingling in the pouch on his hip, Wil turned for home with a spring in his step. There were still a few swallows gathered around the dome of St Paul's Cathedral, still a few weeks to get home in time for Eglwyswrw Fair.

Public Enemy No.1

PART 2

It may have been Bryan Humphreys' intention to get work as a cowboy when he arrived in America, but there was to be no riding the range for him. The big city soon swallowed him up and he turned to drink and gambling. So it was left to the seven-year-old Llewelyn to become the breadwinner for the family. He became a newsboy selling newspapers on the city's corners.

However, selling newspapers on the corners of a city like Chicago was a dangerous business.

The city was full of competing gangs, it was the time of the birth of the Mafia, and every bit of territory, even street corners, was fought over. No surprise then that by the time he was 13, Llewelyn found himself in trouble and in the court of Judge Murray. History does not tell us exactly what Llewelyn had done, but we do know that the judge was so impressed by the boy, by the way he dressed, spoke and defended himself in court, that he took a keen interest in Llewelyn afterwards. Indeed, he virtually adopted him, paying for the best education that money could buy and giving Llewelyn his own name – Murray.

Llewelyn was bright and took to education. Eventually, he became a lawyer, but it seems not for any high ideals regarding law and justice. Rather, having become highly skilled in legal matters, Llewelyn knew just how to manipulate the law in order to help his friends in the Mob. His success was such that he rose quickly through the ranks of the Mafia, soon becoming indispensable to America's Public Enemy No.1, Al 'Scarface' Capone.

4

Craig y Ddinas

As Wil was walking across Blackfriars Bridge, a funny little fellow suddenly jumped out of nowhere.

He had a little goatee beard, wire-rimmed spectacles and a hat woven from bulrushes. 'What's your name?' he demanded.

'The name my father gave me,' Wil said, not liking his manner.

'Where are you from?'

'The place I was born.'

'And where did you get that stick from?'

'The tree I cut it from. What's it to you?' Wil brandished the ash stick in the hope it would make the strange little fellow go away. But it only seemed to excite his interest more.

'Listen, please? I mean no harm, Wil. Only, if you can show me the tree that you cut that stick from, then I can show you great treasures.'

Surprised by the mention of his own name, Wil peered at the little fellow more closely. Suddenly, he recognised him for who he was: a *dyn hysbys*, a cunning man, a wizard.

What harm could it do? Wil asked himself. The place where he'd cut the stick was on his way home and he still had enough time to go there before the Eglwyswrw Fair. Besides, if he could turn the coins half filling the leather pouch into something more, that would be good, wouldn't it?

So Wil agreed, and he and the *dyn hysbys* set off together. For the next week they travelled west, down through the Cotswolds and crossed the river Severn at Gloucester. Then they skirted the Brecon Beacons until they came to a place in the Vale of Neath where two rivers meet. In the fork between them, thrusting out of the earth, was 150 feet of bare rock, turned brown by the sunlight: Craig y Ddinas.

Wil led the *dyn hysbys* up the path to the top.

'There,' he said, pointing at an old ash tree. 'That is where I got my stick.'

'Then help me.' The little fellow was already tearing away at the grass at the base of the trunk.

Together they lifted the turf, dug out the earth between the roots, ripped the tree from the earth, then scraped away at the gravel beneath until they uncovered a large, flat stone. Slipping their fingers under it, they prised the stone up to reveal a set of stone steps descending away into the darkness below.

As Wil went down the steps, he could feel where they had been worn away by many feet over what must have been hundreds of years. As Wil followed the *dyn hysbys* down the dark passage, flames sprang up on torches that were attached to the walls.

At the end of the passage hung an enormous bell, black with age and with a clapper as thick as a tree trunk.

The *dyn hysbys* turned back to Wil and hissed, 'Don't touch the bell!'

Squeezing around it, Wil found himself in a vast cavern. More flames sprang up on torches attached to the walls. The floor was covered with hundreds of sleeping men. Each wore a tunic of burnished armour. Each had a sword or a spear at his side and each had a shield. The way the light flickered off the metal, it was as though there were a thousand torches in the place.

Wil stepped carefully over each sleeping man, being sure not to wake him, as he followed the *dyn hysbys* deeper and deeper into the cavern. When they finally stopped, it was in front of a lone figure seated on a wooden throne. His bearded chin was asleep on his chest and the crown on his head was encrusted with so many jewels that it seemed to throw out a light of its own.

'King Arthur,' whispered the *dyn hysbys*, 'and his sleeping warriors. They await the time when the black eagle and the gold eagle will go to war. Then, they will arise and defeat the enemies of Cymru.'

'Now,' he said, pointing to two piles of coins, one of silver and one of gold, that lay beside the throne. 'You may take from one pile or the other, but not both. And, if you take my advice, you will take only what you need.'

Wil did not need to think about it. He went

straight to the pile of gold coins and filled the leather pouch on his hip to the top. Then, stepping over each sleeping man, he followed the *dyn hysbys* back out of the cavern. But, as he squeezed back around the bell, he was so intent on catching one last glimpse of the sleeping warriors that the pouch on his hip struck the bell.

'D-O-I-N-G!'

There was a clanking and a clattering as warrior after warrior stood up. From somewhere deep in the cavern a voice boomed, 'Has the day come?'

From behind Wil in the passage the *dyn hysbys* answered, 'No, brave soul. The morning of Wales has not yet dawned. Sleep on.'

There was a clanking and a clattering as warrior after warrior lay back down to sleep.

Wil hurried after the *dyn hysbys*, along the passage and up the steps. They replaced the flat stone, the gravel, the tree, the earth between the roots and the turf.

When all was done, the *dyn hysbys* turned to Wil and said, 'Now, you surely have enough to last you a lifetime. However, if some misfortune should befall you and you return, remember, do not touch the bell! But if you do, then remember the words I spoke.' And with that, he disappeared. Not even a puff of smoke was left.

That evening Wil went to a local tavern. He ate well, he drank well, and he slept well and the next morning he set off for Moylgrove and Megan.

The leather purse on his hip was full of gold coins. Enough to buy his brothers out. Enough to replace the dead ox and fix the hole in the farm house roof. Enough to buy Megan a blue dress, a new dresser for the kitchen, and not just a milk cow but a whole herd. And never mind the butter churn, they could afford a dairy maid to turn it and a dairyman to milk the cows.

Of course, thinking of Megan made him wonder again what she had said to the *Tylwyth Teg*, a clean yard or a dirty yard? And how she only ever answered, 'I'm not telling.'

He hadn't walked very far when a thought struck him; he might never come this way again, and in the cavern lay all those riches!

Never mind a dairyman and a dairy maid or fixing the roof, if he went back they could build a new house with a dairy beside it. They could have servants to look after them. They could live like the *crachach* – the gentry!

Wil turned around and went back to Craig y Ddinas. He removed the tree, squeezed past the bell, stepped over the warriors, and filled the deep pockets in his drover's coat so that they were full to bursting with gold and silver. The coat was so heavy that he could hardly lift his legs as stepped back over the sleeping men. The pockets were so full that as he squeezed back around the bell: 'D-O-I-N-G!'

There was a clanking and a clattering as warrior after warrior stood up. From somewhere deep in the cavern a voice boomed, 'Has the day come?'

Wil answered, 'No, sleeping men. It is not time yet. Go back to sleep.'

Even as they were coming out of his mouth, he knew they were the wrong words.

Before he could move, the warriors were on him. Gauntleted fists and the pommels at the end of sword handles struck him. Everything went black.

When Wil awoke, it was to see blue sky and clouds above him. As his head cleared, he found he was on top of Craig y Ddinas. His coat was gone. His hat was gone. His stick was gone. And, worst of all, the leather pouch on his hip was gone. He looked around for the tree that marked the entrance to the cavern, but it was gone too. For hours he searched around in the grass but could find no sign of where it had been.

He wept. No money to buy his brothers out, and the Eglwyswrw Fair only days away; no point going back to Moylgrove. Megan was lost to him.

Public Enemy No.1

PART 3

Llewelyn Murray Humphreys became Al Capone's right-hand man, his top advisor and legal representative. To Capone, he was always Murray the Hump because, apparently, his boss found it impossible to pronounce either Llewelyn or Humphreys correctly. But whatever the truth of the matter, Llewelyn proved effective at his job. For years he managed to keep America's Public Enemy No.1 out of prison. And, when the law finally caught up with

Capone, he was not sentenced for extortion or bank robbery or murder, but for tax evasion.

After that, it was Llewelyn who was to become Public Enemy No.1. Following Al Capone's imprisonment, he realised that the Mob needed to do something with all the dirty money it had. In order to make the money legitimate, he began buying up launderettes – and so it is thanks to him that we now have the expression, 'to launder money'.

Once the money was clean, he looked for other ways to invest it. Llewelyn was among the first to open hotels and casinos in the deserts of Las Vegas. During the 1940s and 50s it was said that this Welshman reputedly controlled the purse strings of major film studios in America. It is strange to think that stars of the silver screen at the time may have been in the employ of this son of Powys farmers.

In 1963 Llewelyn decided he wanted to visit his family home in the hills above Carno. How important this was to him is revealed by the fact that as soon as the plane touched down in London, he got in a taxi and drove straight to Wales.

5

The Ghost Ship

With nothing to go back to Moylgrove for, Wil spent the winter wandering the fields and hills, the lanes and forests of south Wales. Travelling ever westward, by the spring he'd arrived in Tenby. He found work, tending a flock of sheep outside the town walls. Not that he had much use for the money he was paid once he'd eaten and paid for his lodgings. So he just put it aside and forgot about it.

Then, one day in May, a strange and terrible wind began to blow out of the east. The sky turned an angry grey. The sea began to heave with huge, white-topped waves. By mid-afternoon word had gone around the town that a strange ship and been spotted out in the bay.

The townspeople began to gather on Castle Hill. Sure enough, there it was, the strange ship, the wind driving it towards the town, the sea tossing it about as if it were no more than a stick. As it came closer, they could see that its sails were in tatters and it seemed that there was no life on board.

Then, in the dim light of dusk, the first strange lights, flickering and dancing along the decks, were seen.

Word spread through the crowd: 'A ghost ship!' When the strange ship was lost to the darkness, the wailing began. High pitched, spine-tingling, soul-freezing, it drowned out the howling of the gale.

That night, no one in the town slept much. But by morning, the storm had blown itself out.

People began to make their way down to North Beach, where they expected to find the wreckage of the ship. But there wasn't a rope, a cask or even a splintered spar to be seen. The only thing on the beach was a body.

It lay near Goscar Rock, all dressed in black with a long black beard and a gold earring. They thought it dead, until someone tapped it with a foot and suddenly it juddered and spewed out a fountain of sea water.

Some kind souls took pity on the strange

sailor and helped him to their house. Though they nursed him for several days, he said nothing and, as soon as he was strong enough, he left without a single word of thanks.

He made his way through the town and down onto Castle Beach. Perhaps it was the fact that twice a day the tide cut St Catherine's Island off from rest of the town that attracted him to the place. At any rate, it was there on the far side of the island that the strange sailor made his home.

Rumours soon began. Some said that he lived on nothing but live fish that he caught with his bare hands. Others, that each evening he would catch puffins as they returned to their burrows with an old fishing net attached to a pole and that he ate nothing but the breast meat.

Whatever the truth of the matter, Wil found himself drawn to the man. So one afternoon, when the tide was out, he climbed onto the island and made his way around to the seaward side. There he found the strange figure crouched on the rocks, his bearded chin resting on his clenched fists, staring out to sea.

Not knowing what to do, Wil just began to talk. Not to the man in particular, just out loud. He talked of this and that, and then of all that had happened to him. At the mention of Megan and how he'd lost her, the strange sailor suddenly became animated.

'I used to be a pirate captain,' he said, turning his wild eyes towards Wil. 'But I killed the only woman I ever loved in a fit of jealousy. It was after that that the strange wind began to blow. The ship was beyond my control. On and on it drove us. One by one my crew were killed. From accident, disease, murder and worse, until I was the only one left alive. Though the tortured and haunted spirits of my shipmates never left me. Month after month the gale blew us on until I was wrecked upon the beach. But, since I've been here,' he said turning away from Wil and going back to his staring, 'I see the sirens sometimes, between the waves, telling me that my love is all right.'

Wil looked but could see nothing other than the gently rolling sea.

'Do you not see them?' the strange sailor suddenly jumped up and pointed. 'What's that,

my love? Yes! Yes! I'm coming.' And with that, he leapt from the rocks and was gone.

For a moment, Wil gazed in shock and confusion at the place where the sailor had disappeared beneath the water. But then, strangely, an idea came to him. An idea about how he might still win Megan back.

Public Enemy No.1

PART 4

When the taxi finally pulled up outside the Humphreys family home above Carno, he discovered that the place, though a little more dilapidated, was very much as his mother had always described it to him. The tenant farmers still found life extremely hard and the landlords were still forever increasing the rent.

It is easy for us, with email and Skype and Facetime, to forget what emigrating must have meant back then. To leave all you knew and loved, never expecting to see it again. For Llewelyn, this place had only ever existed for him in his mother's stories. But we can see from Llewelyn's actions just how much it meant to him to be there in person.

It was the custom on quarter days, one of the four days of the year when rent was due, for the tenants of the farms to go down to the town to see the landlord's solicitor in order to pay their rent. A few years after Llewelyn's visit, when the tenants went to pay the rent, things did not go as usual.

When each tenant went into the solicitor's office and tried to hand over the money, it was refused. Instead, the solicitor handed them a brown envelope with their name and the address of the farm they rented written on it. Many a heart must have skipped a beat that day, for it was not unusual for a tenant to be given notice to vacate in that manner. However, when the tenants opened the envelopes, they found inside all the papers and deeds necessary for them to have ownership of their farms. All they had to do was sign on the dotted line.

It seems that Llewelyn Murray Humphreys was so moved by his visit that afterwards he had gone to London, bought the whole estate, and was now gifting each farm to the tenants who currently worked it.

A lovely and moving story... as long as we do not dwell on how the money that paid for this generous act was made.

6

Return to Moylgrove

Wil took the little bit of money that he had been putting aside and bought two coal-black Welsh Black cattle. They were not the best, but they would do. Then he set off, not to the east and the cattle markets of England, but north towards Moylgrove.

When his brothers saw Wil coming into the yard driving two black beasts before him, they were terrified. They thought he had returned from hell to haunt them. But Wil spoke so kindly, so calmly that they began to forget their fears. Wil spoke so kindly, so calmly even though as he stood there he saw the ring on Megan's finger as she came out to sweep the step.

'Where have you been?' asked Tomos.

'Oh, brothers! You did me a favour when you threw me off the cliff.'

'What do you mean? asked Sion.

'Well, after you threw me off, I sank all the way to the bottom and found herds and herds of these black beasts roaming about down there.'

'You never did!' said Tom.

'What do they eat down there?' asked Sion.

'Grass,' said Wil. 'Much the same as here, they like it where it grows best in the deepest valleys. I could only catch a couple because I was on my own. But I reckon two of you could catch a whole herd. I could show you if you like?'

'Yes! Show us,' Tom and Sion said together.

Wil led them up and over the top field to the cliffs above Ceibwr Bay.

Standing on the edge, he pointed down at the sea and said, 'That's where I got them.'

Now, what he pointed at was in fact a bed of kelp, great clumps of seaweed swaying lazily in the current. But what his brothers saw were the shadowy figures of herds and herds of black cattle moving across the prairie grass lands at the bottom of the sea.

'I see them!' shouted Tom, the greed written all over his face. And, without another word, he leapt off the cliff.

There was a splash and then a gurgling noise.

'What's that?' asked Sion.

'That's the sound of him laughing. You better get after him or he'll get all the best ones for himself.'

'Wait for me!' shouted Sion, the stupidity

written all over his face. And, without another word, he leapt of the cliff.

There was a splash.

The next day found Wil up on the top field driving two coal-black cattle before the plough as the sole owner of a small farm near Moylgrove in the Wild, Wild West of Wales.

And, following a decent interval, because Megan had been recently widowed, there was a wedding, after which there were many years of happy and prosperous marriage.

Though, even when he was an old, old man and leaning on his stick, Wil would still sometimes ask Megan what she had said to the *Tylwyth Teg*: 'A clean yard or a dirty yard?'

But she would only ever answer, 'I'm not telling!'

But if I tell you that their farm yard was always hoof-deep in manure, and ask you to consider how many coal-black, Welsh Black cattle you think it would have taken for that to always be the case, you may well be able to work it out for yourself.

∽

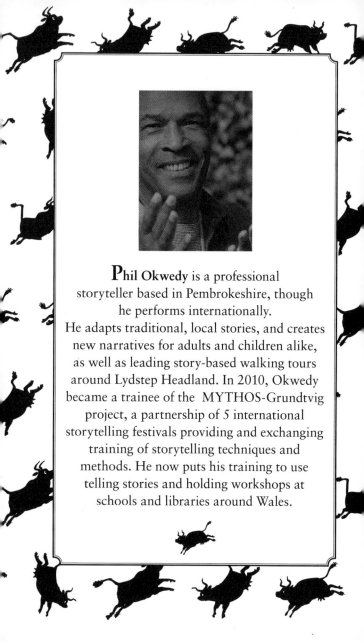

Phil Okwedy is a professional storyteller based in Pembrokeshire, though he performs internationally.
He adapts traditional, local stories, and creates new narratives for adults and children alike, as well as leading story-based walking tours around Lydstep Headland. In 2010, Okwedy became a trainee of the MYTHOS-Grundtvig project, a partnership of 5 international storytelling festivals providing and exchanging training of storytelling techniques and methods. He now puts his training to use telling stories and holding workshops at schools and libraries around Wales.